Dear Parents:

Congratulations! Your child is taking the first steps on an exciting journey. The destination? Independent reading!

STEP INTO READING® will help your child get there. The program offers five steps to reading success. Each step includes fun stories and colorful art or photographs. In addition to original fiction and books with favorite characters, there are Step into Reading Non-Fiction Readers, Phonics Readers and Boxed Sets, Sticker Readers, and Comic Readers—a complete literacy program with something to interest every child.

Learning to Read, Step by Step!

Ready to Read   Preschool–Kindergarten
• big type and easy words • rhyme and rhythm • picture clues
For children who know the alphabet and are eager to begin reading.

Reading with Help   Preschool–Grade 1
• basic vocabulary • short sentences • simple stories
For children who recognize familiar words and sound out new words with help.

Reading on Your Own   Grades 1–3
• engaging characters • easy-to-follow plots • popular topics
For children who are ready to read on their own.

Reading Paragraphs   Grades 2–3
• challenging vocabulary • short paragraphs • exciting stories
For newly independent readers who read simple sentences with confidence.

Ready for Chapters   Grades 2–4
• chapters • longer paragraphs • full-color art
For children who want to take the plunge into chapter books but still like colorful pictures.

STEP INTO READING® is designed to give every child a successful reading experience. The grade levels are only guides; children will progress through the steps at their own speed, developing confidence in their reading.

Remember, a lifetime love of reading starts with a single step!

Step into Reading, Random House, and the Random House colophon are registered trademarks of Penguin Random House LLC.

Visit us on the Web!
StepIntoReading.com
rhcbooks.com

Educators and librarians, for a variety of teaching tools, visit us at RHTeachersLibrarians.com

ISBN 978-0-7364-4310-4 (trade) — ISBN 978-0-7364-9028-3 (lib. bdg.)
ISBN 978-0-7364-4311-1 (ebook)

Printed in the United States of America

10 9 8 7 6 5 4 3 2 1

DISNEY
PRINCESS

Palace
Pets

Tiana's Kind Pony

by Amy Sky Koster

illustrated by the Disney Storybook Art Team

Random House 🏠 New York

Meet Bayou!

She is a pony.

Naveen's parents
give Bayou
to Princess Tiana.

There is a parade
in the town.
Tiana finds Bayou
a costume.

Bayou is shy.
Tiana gives Bayou
a piece of pie.
Yummy!

Tiana takes Bayou
to the parade.
Bayou is happy!

They sit in Tiana's car
and watch the parade.

Now Bayou and Tiana
join the parade.
The crowd cheers.
Bayou has fun!

The next day,
Bayou meets Charlotte.
Charlotte loves
Tiana's kind pony!

Tiana takes Bayou
to Tiana's Palace.
It is Bayou's
favorite place!

Bayou goes with Tiana
to work every day.

14

She plays with
her friend Lily.

Naveen tells Tiana
that Louis is missing.
Louis plays the trumpet.
The band cannot play
without Louis!

Bayou and Lily will help!

They search for Louis.

Lily's tail brushes
some leaves.
Swish, swish, swish!

Bayou's hooves tap
on the sidewalk.
Tap, tap, tap!

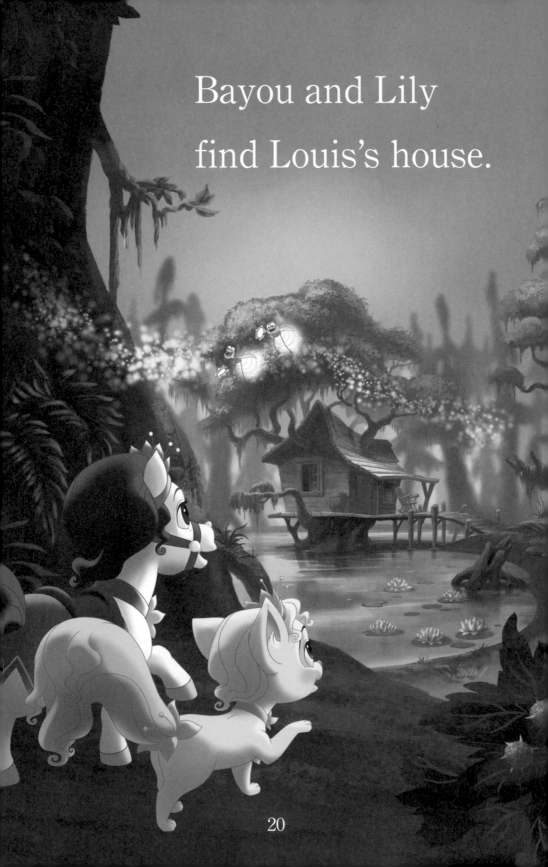

Bayou and Lily
find Louis's house.

Louis is asleep!

Swish, tap. Swish, tap.

Louis hears Lily
and Bayou.

He wakes up!

Louis jumps out of bed.

He grabs his trumpet.

It is time to go!

They all run back
to Tiana's Palace.
Tiana is happy.
Now the band can play!

Tiana thanks
Bayou and Lily.
They are her kind
Palace Pets!